THE FISH WITH THE
DEEP SEA
SMILE

THE FISH WITH THE DEEP SEA SMILE

Stories and Poems for Reading to
Young Children

by
Margaret Wise Brown

Illustrated by
Roberta Rauch

Delacorte Press

Published by
Bantam Doubleday Dell Books for Young Readers
Bantam Doubleday Dell Publishing Group, Inc.
1540 Broadway
New York, New York 10036

The trademark Delacorte Press® is registered in the U.S. Patent and
Trademark Office.

ISBN: 0-385-31112-5

Reprinted by arrangement with The Shoe String Press

Printed in the United States of America

December 1993

10 9 8 7 6 5 4 3 2 1

TO

LUCY SPRAGUE MITCHELL

CONTENTS

STORIES   PAGE

THE SHY LITTLE HORSE 11

THE FISH WITH THE DEEP SEA SMILE . . 16

THE GOOD LITTLE BAD LITTLE PIG . . . 18

ADVENTURE IN THE SPRING 23

THE STEAM ROLLER: A FANTASY . . . 25

THE CHILD'S GARDEN 32

THE GARDEN 33

THOSE CRAZY CROWS 39

THE WILD BLACK CROWS 39

SNEAKERS, THAT RAPSCALLION CAT . . . 40

    SNEAKERS COMES TO TOWN 44

    THE SKY FOLLOWS SNEAKERS TO TOWN . . 47

    SNEAKERS AND THE EASTER FLOWERS . . 51

    THE EASTER SURPRISE 53

    SNEAKERS AND THE EASTER BUNNIES . . 54

    THE COUNTRY HAPPENS TO SNEAKERS AGAIN 60

THE DEAD BIRD 62

HOW DO YOU KNOW IT'S SPRING? . . . 64

THE FIERCE YELLOW PUMPKIN 65

FALL OF THE YEAR 70

CHRISTMAS EVE 71

BUGS 74

FISH 75

CONTENTS

STORIES   PAGE

HOW THE LITTLE CITY BOY CHANGED PLACES
   WITH THE LITTLE COUNTRY BOY FOR A
   YEAR 76

THE SONGS THAT ARE SUNG TO AN AEROPLANE 82

THE RAT THAT SAID BOO TO THE CAT . . 84

THE CHILDREN'S CLOCK 87

LITTLE LOST KITTEN 90

THE LITTLE GIRL'S MEDICINE 91

SLEEPY STORIES

LITTLE DONKEY CLOSE YOUR EYES . . . 99

THE POLITE LITTLE POLAR BEAR . . . 101

LITTLE BROWN TUG 105

THE WONDERFUL KITTEN 106

FISH SONG 111

THE BOYS WHO FLEW AWAY: A DREAM . . 112

WHEN I SHUT MY EYES 113

THE WILD BLACK CROWS—A CIRCULAR SONG . 114

THE LITTLE BLACK CAT WHO WENT TO
   MATTITUCK 115

FOUR FISHING BOATS 121

THE PALE BLUE FLOWER 122

ABOUT A LITTLE MOUSE NAMED HENRY FRITZELL 124

THE WONDERFUL DAY 126

THE HEAVENLY DAY 128

STORIES

THE SHY LITTLE HORSE

Once upon a time in a barnyard there was a shy little horse. Every time he heard anyone coming, he ran away. Not so the donkey, not so the pig.

The old gray donkey rolled his eyes and lowered his head, put forward his ears, and then he trotted over to see who the visitor was. And the old fat pig, if she wasn't eating, wallowed over to the side of her pen and grunted at the visitor. But the little horse was shy. He kicked up his heels and he lowered his head and he galloped across the fields away from the visitor.

He galloped away and his mother galloped with him to the far end of the field where the grass was wet and green from the stream that flowed there.

Then one day a visitor came to the barnyard. The visitor was a tall man with a mustache.

The donkey saw him coming and ran to the fence and stuck forward his long ears and rolled his big brown jackrabbit eyes. But the visitor didn't pay any attention to the donkey. The old pig blinked at him, and the chickens scratched about as though there were only chickens in the barnyard. But the visitor didn't even see the old pig and the chickens. The visitor was looking at the shy little horse.

And that shy little horse just lowered his head and kicked up his heels and galloped away.

Now this visitor had come just to see the shy little horse. That was why he came to the barnyard. So he climbed the fence and walked across the field after the little horse. But every time the man got near him, the little horse kicked up his heels and tossed his head in the air and away he flew across the field. And his mother galloped with him and stayed by his side.

But the tall man with the moustache knew a lot about shy little horses because he loved them. He had watched horses for a long time. He knew that the shy little horse was also a curious little horse, just chock full of curiosity. So he just went and leaned against the fence and whistled away to himself and didn't look at the shy little horse any more.

Now that funny little horse saw the man do this and he heard him whistling; because the shy little horse had brand new eyes and brand new ears, and he heard and saw everything. He lowered his head and nibbled the green grass. But while he was nibbling he peeked at the man and pricked up his ears to hear the man whistling. The man didn't move and kept on whistling. The shy little horse kicked up his heels and ran farther down the field and nibbled some more grass and peeked at the man. The man didn't move and kept on whistling. Then the shy little horse nibbled some grass nearer to the man. The man didn't move and kept on whistling. What a funny man, thought the shy little horse. Why doesn't he chase me and try to get me in a corner and put a halter over my head? The man didn't move and kept on whistling. The little horse nibbled nearer and nearer. The man didn't move and kept on whistling. The shy little horse's mother put forward her ears and looked hard at the man. Then she snorted and whinnied and kicked up her heels and galloped far away around the edge of the field. The shy little horse tossed his brand new head in the air and galloped with her. They circled around the field and stopped even nearer to the man than they had been before and nibbled the green grass. The man didn't move and kept on whistling.

By this time the little horse was so curious he was nearly popping inside. He had never seen a man like this before. All the other men had chased him into a corner and caught him and put a halter over his head. The man didn't move and kept on whistling. The shy little horse stepped nearer and nearer. He was quite near to the man now, and he stood there ready to leap away and gallop to the far ends of the field. The man didn't move and kept on whistling. The shy little horse nosed nearer and nearer. The whistling tickled his ears in a way he liked. And he liked the man to stand so still he could get a good look at him. And he liked the quiet way of the man.

Then the man moved just a tiny little bit. If the shy little horse hadn't been looking so hard, he wouldn't have seen. The man uncurled his fingers, and on the palm of his hand were two white square lumps. The

13

little horse stood there ready to jump away if the man moved any more. The man didn't move and kept on whistling. The shy little horse's mother stretched her head forward to make sure that she saw what she saw. For on the man's hand were two white square lumps of sugar. Just what the old horse loved, and her mouth began to water as she thought of the sweet prickly taste of sugar. She had been out in the field nibbling green grass for so long with her little horse that no one had given her any sugar. She stepped nearer to the man, almost right up to him. The man didn't move and kept on whistling. This was a wonderful thing. The old mother horse stepped right up to the man and buried her nose in his hand and took one lump of sugar and stepped back and chewed it. Then she stepped up and took the other lump of sugar. The man didn't move and kept on whistling. Then after a while he walked out of the field the way he had come and went away.

The next day he came back, and he stood there whistling and he gave the mother horse another lump of sugar. The third day when he came, he walked right over to the mother horse and put a halter over her head and gave her a lump of sugar. Then he led her out of the field, and the shy little horse followed after, close to his mother's side. The man led the mother horse and the shy little horse through the barn-yard among the chickens, past the old fat pig who was eating potato peelings, past the old gray donkey who was eating thistle and staring with his big jackrabbit eyes. The man led the mother horse and the shy little horse right down the road where the little horse had never been before. His brand new hooves made a clicking noise on the road as he trotted along beside his mother. And the shy little horse was delighted.

Way down the road they went, until they came to a small dirt road. The man turned up the dirt road, and the shy little horse's brand new hooves didn't make clicking noises any more on the dirt, they just made soft little thuds. They went up the dirt road to a long white house with a big white stable with green doors and windows, all green and white. And there were buckets painted green and white, too, in stripes.

And out from the house came a shy little boy and looked at the shy little horse.

For the tall man with the moustache was the father of the shy little boy, and he had bought the shy little horse for the little boy's very own. The little boy's mother came out of the house and said what a beautiful young horse it was. And the little boy said, "Some day I will ride him."

It wasn't so long before the shy little boy had taught the shy little horse to eat sugar out of his own hand. And the shy little horse and the shy little boy grew up together, and it wasn't long—maybe a year or two, for there was plenty of time—before the little boy had grown old enough to ride the shy little horse and the shy little horse had grown large enough to carry the little boy on his back.

They rode all over the country, the boy and his horse, and after a while they weren't even shy any more. They jumped fences and galloped across the green grassy fields.

THE FISH WITH THE DEEP
SEA SMILE

They fished and they fished
Way down in the sea
Down in the sea a mile
They fished among all the fish in the sea
For the fish with the deep sea smile.

One fish came up from the deep of the sea
From down in the sea a mile
It had blue green eyes
And whiskers three
But never a deep sea smile.

One fish came up from the deep of the sea
From down in the sea a mile
With electric lights up and down his tail
But never a deep sea smile.

They fished and they fished
Way down in the sea
Down in the sea a mile
They fished among all the fish in the sea
For the fish with the deep sea smile.

One fish came up with terrible teeth
One fish with long strong jaws
One fish came up with long stalked eyes
One fish with terrible claws.

They fished all through the ocean deep
For many and many a mile
And they caught a fish with a laughing eye
But none with a deep sea smile.

And then one day they got a pull
From down in the sea a mile
And when they pulled the fish into the boat
HE SMILED A DEEP SEA SMILE.

And as he smiled, the hook got free
And then, what a deep sea smile!
He flipped his tail and swam away
Down in the sea a mile.

THE GOOD LITTLE BAD LITTLE PIG

Poor little pig. He lived in a muddy pigpen, in an old pigpen of garbage and mud, with four other little pigs and an old mother sow. He was a little white-pink pig, but the mud all over him made him look pink and black and gray-pink.

Then one day a little boy named Peter asked his mother if he could have a pig.

"What!" said Peter's mother. "You want a dirty little bad little pig?"

She was very surprised.

"No," said Peter. "I want a clean little pig. And I don't want a bad little pig. And I don't want a good little pig. I want a good little bad little pig."

"But I never heard of a clean little pig," said Peter's mother. "Still, we can always try to find one."

So they sent the farmer who owned the pig a telegram:

"Farmer, Farmer
I want a pig
Not too little
And not too big
Not too good
And not too bad
The very best pig
That the mother pig had."

The farmer read the telegram, and then he went out to the pigpen and looked at the five little pigs. Three little pigs were fast asleep. "Those," said the farmer, "are good little pigs." And one little pig was jumping all around. "That," said the farmer, "is a bad little pig." And then he heard a little pig squeak, and then he heard a little pig squeal. But when he looked, there was just one little gray-pink pig standing on an old tin pan in the corner of the pen. "That," said the farmer, "is a good little bad little pig." And he reached in and grabbed the little pig by the hind legs and put him in a box and sent him by train to Peter.

When the express man brought the little pig to Peter's front door, his mother said, "What a dirty little pig!" And the pig said, "Squeak squeeeeeeeeeeeee ump ump ump." And Peter said, "Wait till I give this little pig a bath." But when they let the little pig out, he ran all over the room squealing like a fire engine.

"What a bad little pig!" said Peter's father, and he had to catch the little pig by the hind leg to make him hold still while Peter put the red leather dog harness around the little pig's stomach.

"Wait," said Peter, "until the little pig knows us.

He is not a bad little pig." And he clipped a red leather leash on the little pig's harness.

The little pig stared at Peter out of his blue squint eyes, and then he shook himself and trotted after Peter on the leash.

"What a good little pig!" said Peter's mother, as she came in the room with a pan of bread and milk for the little pig to eat after his journey.

"Wait," said Peter. "Remember this is a good little bad little pig."

"Galump gump gump gump gump." The little pig was eating. He seemed to be snuffling and sneezing into his food as he ate.

"What a bad little pig!" said the cook, who had come in to see how the little pig was enjoying the bread and milk. "What terrible eating manners he has!"

"But he does enjoy his food," said the little boy.

"Yes," said the cook, "he does enjoy his food." And she beamed with a smile all over, for the cook did dearly love for anyone to enjoy his food. "What a good little pig," she said. "He has eaten up everything in the pan."

"Come on, you good little bad little gray-pink pig," said Peter. "I will give you a bath so you will be a clean little white-pink pig."

So Peter and his mother and his father and the cook all went into the bathroom and put the little pig right into the bathtub and let the warm water run all over him. The little pig squeaked and squealed and wiggled all around. But Peter's mother held his

20

front legs and his father held the little pig's hind legs, so that the little pig couldn't kick himself or the people who were bathing him. The little boy took a big cake of white soap and rubbed it all along the pig's back until he was all covered with pure white soapsuds. Then he took a scrubbing brush, and he scrubbed and he scrubbed right down through the bristles on the little pig's back to the little pig's skin. He scrubbed and he scrubbed until the pure white soapsuds were all black and gray. Then he poured warm water over the pig's back until there was no soap on it. Then he put some more soapsuds all over the little pig's back. And he scrubbed and he scrubbed and he scrubbed and he scrubbed and he scrubbed until the pure white soapsuds were all gray and black again. Then he rinsed off the pig's back with warm water and put more soapsuds on. But this time the soapsuds stayed almost pure white. So he left them on the little pig's back and washed his stomach and his feet until he was all clean and white and pink from the tip of his tail to the tip of his nose. Then they dried the little pig with a great big bath towel, and Peter took him for a walk in the sunshine.

"Look," said Peter as he showed his little pig to the policeman on the corner. "Did you ever see such a fine little clean little pig?"

"I never did," said the policeman, "see such a good little pig." And he blew his whistle and stopped all the automobiles so that Peter and the little pig could get across the street.

But the little pig did not want to get across, and he

pulled back on the red leather leash and refused to budge. Peter pulled and he pulled, but the little pig would not go across the street.

"What a bad little pig!" said the people in the automobiles, and they began to honk their horns. And the little pig began to squeal and squeak. "Squeak squeee-eeeee ump ump ump." But the policeman held up his hand and wouldn't let the automobiles go. Then he came over to Peter and his pig.

"You pull him, Peter," he said, "and I'll get behind him and push." So they did. And when they got to the middle of the road, the little pig trotted on after Peter just as nice as you please. "What a good little pig," said the people on the other side of the street.

And so it was that Peter got just what he wanted. A good little bad little pig. Sometimes the little pig was good and sometimes he was bad, but he was the best little pig that a little boy ever had.

ADVENTURE IN THE SPRING

I went walking out in the world
To see what I could find
I went walking out in the world
And left the house behind
And this is what I found
A little gray bird on four green eggs
The eggs didn't make a sound
I found
Bright red cherries shining on a tree
Red as rubies there for me
And amber cherry gum bubbling
    through the bark
And then I heard a meadowlark
Hiding somewhere in the grass
Singing of Spring as I went past
I found
A dark wet swamp
With dark black mud
And there in the swamp
A golden bud
The first marigold
More yellow than gold
Growing for me in the swamp

The grass was green the grass was
    bright
Day seemed forever
There was no night
The sun was yellow
The air was light
It was the Spring I found.

THE STEAM ROLLER
(*A Fantasy*)

A Silly Story!

Once there was a little girl and it was Christmas. It was Christmas and her mother and father didn't give her any oranges for Christmas. No dolls. No candy. No new clothes, no books. No sugar plums, no baby carriages. No!—. They gave her a Steam Roller. A big black steam roller with a silver bell and a brass chimney on it as shiny as gold. Smoke was coming out the chimney and a sort of hissing sound of steam swsss-wssswwwwwsss.

The little girl climbed up the ladder to the driver's seat, pushed the sticks that made the steam roller go, blew the whistle and rang the bell, and away she went down the road. The big steam roller wheel crushed all the little pebbles on the road and squashed all the big rocks.

Crunch, Crunch, Crunch, it went rolling down the road making everything flat before it. And ssssssss a fine smoke of steam came out of its brass chimney and made the steam roller go. There were a lot of buttons to push and sticks to pull. But the little girl didn't know which to push or which to pull to make the steam roller stop.

An old pig went wallowing across the road and blinked its small red eyes.

"Look out old Pig," said the little girl. "Get out of my way because I can't stop.

"Get out of my way or I'll squash you flat."

But the old pig didn't get out of the way. And the steam roller ran right over it and squashed the old pig flat on the road. Flat as a pig's shadow in the middle of the road.

A chicken came fluttering over the road. The little girl blew the steam roller whistle. Screeeeeeeeee—up.

"Get out of my way or I'll squash you flat."

And the old yellow chicken got so excited squawking "Which Way Which Way Which Way," and flapping its yellow feather wings, it flew right under the steam roller. Looking back the little girl saw it flat on the road like the shadow of a chicken or a feather fan.

But the little girl couldn't stop the big steam roller and it went rolling down the road squashing everything in its way. It squashed her mean old aunt flat on the road. It squashed three people she didn't know, it squashed two automobiles and a garbage truck and a trolley car.

Then a policeman stood up in the middle of the road. He held up his hand and blew his whistle. "S T O P," he said.

"I can't stop," said the little girl, for by this time she had forgotten how to stop. And she ran right over the policeman and squashed him flat on the road with his hand in the air saying S T O P.

The road ahead was clear. No one was on it. No Pigs, No Chickens, No Aunts, no people she didn't know, no automobiles, no garbage trucks, no trolley

cars and no policemen. Then along came the little girl's teacher.

"Merry Christmas little girl," said the little girl's teacher. And the little girl said, "Merry Christmas," but the steam roller wouldn't stop and it squashed the teacher and the book she was carrying, right flat in the middle of the road with a Merry Christmas smile on her face. Flat in the road like a shadow.

Then the little girl saw her friends coming down the road, the children that were just her age, and they called to her saying, "Give us a ride on your steam roller."

"Look out," called the little girl. "I can't stop this steam roller and it will squash you flat."

But the children didn't seem to hear her and they came running toward her. The little girl blew the whistle and rang the silver bell, but still the children came running toward her. "STOP" she called to them. But still they came running.

This will never do, thought the little girl. I can't squash all the children my own age. So she headed the steam roller across a field and then she jumped out of it while it was still going. The steam roller went rolling over the field squashing the fences until they looked like the shadows of fences around the fields. And away it went. The little girl hurt herself on the road when she jumped from the steam roller going full speed. But when she got up she found that she hadn't hurt herself very much. It didn't hurt for long.

The children her own age came running up to her. "We wanted a ride," they said.

"Oh, no you didn't," said the little girl. "That steam roller doesn't stop, whatever stick you pull or button you push. And it squashes everything it comes to flat. It would have squashed you all flat if I hadn't headed it off the road into the fields and jumped out."

"Oh," said the children her own age. And they looked after the steam roller. It was just rolling over the last hill. It rolled over the hill and then disappeared into the distance. It rolled off into the ocean and squashed a few fish flat and stopped.

"Well," said the little girl. "I am glad that old steam roller is gone." And she wished the children a Merry Christmas and ran home to her mother and father.

"Well," said her father, "and how did you like your steam roller ride? And what did you do with your steam roller?"

"At first, it was fun," said the little girl, "but I couldn't stop the steam roller and it squashed everything and everybody it came to flat on the road. And then all the children my own age came running up the road and I couldn't squash them, so I headed the steam roller across the fields and jumped out of it while it was going. And the steam roller rolled away across the fields squashing the fences and went away out of sight. It just rolled away.

"And a pig and a chicken – – – – – – –
– – – – – – – –
– –
– –
– – – –
– – – and a policeman

all got squashed flat on the road like shadows and I don't know how to get them up again."

"Well," said the little girl's mother and father. "We have another Christmas present for you."

And there at the front door all wrapped up in tissue paper with red ribbons on it was a giant steam shovel.

"Get in that," said her father and mother, "and go scoop up the squashed flat pigs and people and automobiles. Scoop them up out of their shadows and they won't be squashed flat any more."

So the little girl tore off the tissue paper from the steam shovel and away she went down the road. Off she went on the caterpillar steam shovel wheels and when she came to the pig shadow, Scoop she scooped and the old pig grunted up out of its shadow and trotted away. And when she came to the chicken, Scoop, she scooped it right up out of its shadow; and still cackling, Which Way Which Way Which Way, the chicken fluttered away.

And when she came to her mean old aunt and the three people she didn't know, Scoop she scooped them right out of their shadows and they all went hurrying down the road.

She scooped up the two automobiles and the garbage truck and the trolley car and off they rattled. And Scoop she scooped up the policeman, who raised his other hand and blew his whistle and said Go. Then scoop she scooped up her teacher out of the shadow on the road and her teacher said "Merry Christmas" again and the little girl said "Merry Christmas."

And then all the children her own age came run-

ning and she gave them each a ride up in the air in the
scoop for the fun of it. Scoop she scooped them way
high up in the air and then let them down again.

Then she turned the steam shovel around, and off
she went home to Christmas dinner.

THE CHILD'S GARDEN

In this garden you will find
No columbine or eglantine.
All the flowers you will find
Were found by me and they are mine.
You will find
White violets from the woods
That I dug up in the spring
And you will find
Daisies from the fields
And one buttercup.
I planted lots of buttercup seeds
But only one came up.

THE GARDEN

Once upon a time early in the morning there were two little boys. The birds woke them up early in the morning. There was a soft wind blowing. It was Spring.

It was a fine shining morning, and this is what they did.

They got up and went outdoors to plant a garden. The day before, they had worked all day digging up two big squares of land and making the dirt all soft and even. So this morning the dirt was all soft and dark and brown from the morning dew, and all they had to do was to rake it. There were no hard chunks of dirt or stones left in it. The little boy named Jack found two pink earthworms in his garden, but he left them there because they would wiggle around in the dirt and keep the ground soft. Both Jack and Billy, for that was the other little boy's name, knew that much about gardens even though they had never planted one before. But after they had raked the ground all fine and smooth, they had to sit down on a log and think what they should do next.

"Now it is time to plant something," said Billy.

There was a bottle of little round yellow radish seeds in the tool house, so they both went and took a handful. Then they took a stick and made a little ditch down through the dirt the way their father had done in the big garden. And they dropped the little yellow seeds into the ditch in the dark brown earth. Then they went and sat on the log to try to remember what to do next. While they were sitting there wondering, they heard a CAW CAW CAW overhead, and two great birds with black wings flapping flew right down and started eating the seeds out of their garden.

The little boys clapped their hands and grabbed their rakes and ran at the birds, calling, "Shoo, Crow, Shoo!" Then the birds flapped their big black wings and flew away.

"Now," said Billy, "we will have to build a big fierce scarecrow to frighten those crows away. Come on. I know where an old hat is and where we can find some funny old clothes. We will make a very fierce and funny scarecrow."

"No," said Jack. "That is not the next thing to do. While we are doing that, the crows will come back and eat up all our radish seeds."

Then he remembered what to do.

"Cover up the seeds with dirt first. Don't you remember? We are supposed to cover up the seeds with dirt and then put a stick at each end of the row and a sign on the stick that tells what is planted there."

"Oh, yes," said Billy. "But we ought to build a scarecrow, too."

But first they covered up the seeds with dirt and patted the dirt down with their hands just a little so the ground would be soft enough for the little radish plants to grow through. Then they stuck sticks in the ground at each end of the row, and they put a piece of paper on each stick.

"Now we should write RADISH on the piece of paper," said Jack. "And we don't know how to write."

So they went and sat on the log and thought about what they should do. No one was awake in the house yet. It was still early in the morning.

"I know," said Billy. "We will draw pictures of the radishes on the paper and color them green and red with our crayons."

So they ran and got their crayon box, and that was what they did.

After they had done that, there was a row of radishes planted in each garden. A very straight row and a very neat row and a very fine row.

"Now," said Jack, "We have to plant something else. This is not a radish farm."

And so they went and sat down on the log and thought for a long time.

Then Billy jumped up. "I have an idea!" he said. "What is it?"

"I have an idea, and I won't tell what it is. But I know where I can get all the seeds I want."

"Where?" said Jack.

"I won't tell," said Billy. And he laughed and he laughed and he laughed.

"All right," said Jack. "I know where some wild strawberry plants are in the woods and I will go and dig them all up. And I won't tell you where they are."

But Billy was so busy laughing over his seeds that he didn't pay any attention.

So Jack got a shovel and a basket, and off he went to the woods after wild strawberry plants.

As soon as he was out of sight, Billy jumped up and ran to the kitchen. He was still laughing. "This is easy!" he said. And he climbed up to the kitchen shelves and he opened a can that said OATMEAL. He took a whole handful of the oatmeal grains and put it in his pocket. Then he opened another can and took a handful of rice. Just then he saw a box of raisins. Raisin seeds, thought Billy, and he took some of them. "I will eat the raisins and plant the seeds." Then he took some green peas and some barley and some spaghetti.

Then he climbed down and ran back to his garden and planted each one in a row. He was just drawing the signs and singing OATS AND BEANS AND BARLEY GROW, when Jack came back.

Jack had his basket filled with little green strawberry plants. Some of them had small white flowers with yellow centers. And he had some violet plants too with purple flowers and buds. And he had an idea, too.

He planted three rows of strawberry plants, and he planted the violets along the edge of his garden. Then he got ready to plant his idea. He took a stick and made holes in the dirt as deep as his finger, as far from each other as the length of his foot.

Billy sat on the log and watched him and laughed. "Strawberries and violets! Some vegetable garden! You should see what I'm going to grow in mine. Just wait till mine comes up!"

But Jack didn't pay any attention to Billy. He just went on digging his holes. Then when they were all dug, he went in the house and got some potatoes and dropped one in each of the holes. Then he covered up the holes with dirt and stuck a little stick by each hole.

About that time breakfast was nearly ready, and the little boys' father and mother came out to see what kind of a garden their children had planted.

Jack showed them how he had radishes and potatoes and strawberries and violets planted in his.

Then Billy showed them how he had planted oatmeal and rice and raisins and barley and spaghetti and peas and radishes in his garden.

When they heard about the oatmeal and rice and barley and spaghetti, they laughed and laughed. But all they said was, "We'll see in a month's time what comes up."

37

And their father promised to bring some tomato plants from town that night for them to plant.

Then they all went in to breakfast.

And if you had been Jack or Billy, which garden would you have planted? And what do you think came up?

THOSE CRAZY CROWS

Those crazy crows on ragged wing
Fly over the woods
They never sing
They screech and they scream
But they never sing
Those crazy crows
They never sing

THE WILD BLACK CROWS

Oh the wild black crows, the wild black crows
　Nobody knows, how the wild black crows
Fly far away to where nobody goes
　Where nobody goes and nobody knows
Nobody knows but the wild black crows.

SNEAKERS, THAT RAPSCALLION CAT

Once there was a little fat cat, and his name was Sneakers. His mother called him Sneakers because he had four white paws and the rest of him was inky black. All her other little kittens were inky black all over; so that when his mother saw Sneakers lying on his back waving his four white paws in the air, she thought he must have gone wading in her saucer of milk while she was taking a nap. She picked him out of her pile of kittens by the scruff of his neck, and she lay down, holding him squirming between her two front paws and tried to clean the milk off his tiny feet and make them inky black like all her other kittens' feet. She licked and she licked; and she purred a song, she purred a song while she licked. But the milk would not come off. And she licked and she licked, and she purred and she purred, but still he had four white paws. Just then she saw the little boy come running towards her. It was the first warm day in the year, and he had on a pair of brand-new clean white sneakers. The mother cat looked at the little boy's sneakers, and she looked at the little kitten with its four white paws; and she blinked at the little boy's sneakers, and she blinked at her kitten with its four white paws; and then she purred and she purred and she purred, and the little kitten was called Sneakers from then on.

Now this Sneakers was a rapscallion cat from the time he was born. While the other kittens stayed in the box until they grew up enough, Sneakers was off even before he grew up enough and away after little black bugs, and chasing butterfly shadows across the ground, and pouncing on people's shoelaces if they were the least bit hanging. He went Pounce Pounce Pounce all day long, and then he went pounce into his bed at night; and curling his little white feet under him into a warm fur ball, he went pounce to sleep. His mother always knew that no matter how much he went pouncing off, he would always come pouncing back, so she did not worry about him. But she did think over and over again, "By the incredible velvet that grows on my nose, this is a funny little cat!"

One day his mother licked his little face all clean and smooth, and she said to him, "Now, Sneakers my kitten, my little fur cat, away you go! You are to live in the house with the little boy, and make him laugh, and chase away the mice, and never knock anything off the tables. I am a barn cat, and my home is in the barn here in the hay. But you will be a house cat, and will sleep before the fire and only come out here in the daytime. Now off you go to the house, and keep your little paws clean as the milk that you drink every morning."

So Sneakers went to live in the big house and be the little boy's kitten. At first it seemed very quiet in the house at night, after the barn—the horses stomping in their stalls and the mice squeaking and squealing in the hayloft. Then at table one day, purely by accident, the little boy knocked over a plate of peaches, and they rolled all over the floor in every direction, little round peaches rolling away. "My but I'm glad this happened," thought the funny little kitten as he batted one of the peaches all around the floor. "I do wish that lots of things would come spilling all over the floor for me to chase every day." Everyone laughed so hard at Sneakers scooting around after the peaches with his paw that they forgot who knocked the peaches over. The little boy laughed, too. But the little kitten never knocked things off himself. He just prowled round and round with one eye cocked and waited for things to happen.

One afternoon the cook came back from town all dressed up in a brand new hat—a brand new hat with red feathers on it. She met Sneakers in the pantry.

"Where are you going, you little Sneaker cat?"

"Just *prowling around—prowling around.*"* Sneakers blinked his bright yellow eyes.

Whiff! The wind came blowing in the kitchen door and blew the cook's hat off with all its red feathers.

Pounce! went Sneakers. Pounce on the feathers and the brand new hat. And he slid it across the floor.

"Oh, Sneakers, you kitten, you rapscallion cat! Give me back my brand new hat!"

But Sneakers was having fun, and he knew the cook moved very slowly. He batted the hat with his milk-white paw and thought, MY, BUT I AM GLAD THIS HAPPENED. And he skidded the hat under the table.

* Cat-like sound.

The cook had to chase him all over the kitchen and into the sink before she could get her brand new hat. She put it back on her head, right on top of her head, and stood there. Sneakers just sat by the side of the sink—where he wasn't supposed to be—and licked his milk-white paw.

"Oh, Sneakers," said the cook, "the minute I saw you, I knew you were in here waiting for mischief."

"No," said Sneakers, "I was just *prowling around, prowling around.*" And he walked out of the kitchen on his four white paws to find the little boy.

The little boy was down at the barn making the harnesses soft and clean with saddle soap and a wet sponge.

"Hello, Sneaker cat," said the little boy. "Where are you going?"

"Just *prowling around, prowling around,*" said Sneakers and he rubbed his fur back against the little boy's bare leg. Then he sat down to wait for something to happen—for the sponge to drop or something to spill. For Sneakers was a rapscallion cat.

SNEAKERS COMES TO TOWN

Sneakers went prowling around and prowling around all summer on his sneaker white paws, and he grew from a kitten to a cat. But he was only a small cat the size of a large kitten. And he was still the little boy's cat, and he was still a rapscallion cat. When the little boy caught a fish in the river and pulled it up on the bank, Pounce went Sneakers on the wiggling fish; when the cook's feet went walking by one of Sneaker's hiding places, Pounce came Sneakers, Pounce at the cook's feet; and at night he went pounce to sleep on all the best chairs in the house. He was a rapscallion cat. But the little boy loved him, and he was the little boy's cat.

Then one day at the end of summer the whole house packed up to go to town for the winter. The cook packed her big feather hat; and the little boy's mother packed all the straw hats and all the silver and all the summer clothes; and she packed all the little boy's shorts, and sandals, and sneakers, and socks, and all his clothes; and the little boy's father packed all his pipes, and tobacco, and fishing rods, and all his clothes. And then they all got in the big car with all the suitcases to drive to town.

The little boy was very sad. Sneakers couldn't go. His mother said the city was no place for an animal, and his father said that all animals belonged in the country. And Sneakers couldn't go. He would have to wait all winter for the little boy to come back. So just before the car drove off, the little boy jumped out to tell Sneakers goodbye. He called Sneakers, but the little cat didn't come. He looked all through the house, but Sneakers wasn't there. He looked in the cellar, and he looked in the barn, and he looked in the field behind the barn. No Sneakers.

So the little boy just called out across the field, "Goodbye, my Sneakers, my rapscallion cat."

Then he went back to the car. And the car drove off to the city, and he didn't see Sneakers to tell him goodbye.

When they got to the city, they drove to a red brick house on Fifteenth Street with a very small garden in front of it behind a high iron fence. The garden was the size of a very small rug. It wasn't even big enough to start to run in without bumping into the big iron fence. But Sneakers wasn't there, and the little boy didn't want to run anyway.

His mother and his father and the cook went in the house; and the cook unpacked her feather hat, and his mother unpacked the silver, and his father unpacked his tobacco pipes, and then his mother opened the suitcases to unpack some clothes. First she opened the suitcase with the little boy's toys in it, and some nuts and sticks fell all over the floor. They rolled all over the floor and under the bed.

Then the little boy's mother opened the suitcase with his father's clothes, and unpacked them and hung them up on wooden hangers. Then she opened her own suitcase and hung up all her dresses. Then she opened the little boy's suitcase. And—Wait! What in the world?—out jumped a little black bundle of fur and jumped up on the bed. It was Sneakers. Sneakers purring, and purring, and arching his back. He meowed just once when the little boy ran up to him.

"Oh, that Sneakers, THAT RAPSCALLION CAT!" said the little boy's mother. "How in the world did you get in that suitcase!"

"He must have fallen asleep there and we didn't see him when we closed the bag. Lucky he didn't smother, that bad little cat." The little boy's father puffed on his pipe, but his eyes were smiling.

But the little boy didn't say anything. He just scratched Sneakers on the nose. Sneakers batted the little boy's hand with his white sneaker paw.

"What will we ever do in the city with a rapscallion cat!" said the little boy's mother. "We had better send him back to the country when the car goes back."

"No," said the little boy's father, "If he has come this far all by himself, let him stay."

So the little cat stayed in the city with the little boy.

THE SKY FOLLOWS SNEAKERS TO TOWN

Life in the city was a brand new surprise for
Sneakers. Of course the little boy had been in the city
many times before, so he knew all about it. But
Sneakers didn't. It was all a big surprise to Sneakers.
And so at first he just sat in the window and stared and
stared out of the window. What a funny world it was
for a little country cat! There were tall houses across
the street, taller than the farmhouse and taller than the
barn. They were taller, even, than the trees and the
hills around the farm. From where he sat in the downstairs window of the little boy's house, he couldn't even
see the sky. "Oh my," thought Sneakers, "I hope the
sky didn't get left in the country; and if the sky got
left, where are the birds that flew in the sky?" Across
the street at that moment came a burst of golden light

on the sidewalk, warm golden light on the people walking down the street. The little patches of grass in front of some of the houses grew greener. "My But I'm Glad That Happened," said Sneakers. "The sun has followed me to town. I only wish the trees and the birds had come, too." And just then one little leaf fluttered down the street all by itself. Only one single leaf to show that it was Fall. But it made Sneakers happy. "Good," said Sneakers, "A tree has followed me to town. I only wish the sky had come, too, and all the birds in the sky. I shall miss the sky,"—then he licked his chops—"and I shall miss the birds in the sky."

How the little boy would have laughed if he had known that Sneakers thought there could be a sun without any sky to be in! But Sneakers never thought very long about any one thing if there were other brand new things to think about. By this time he was prowling around the room looking in every corner and under every chair, and sniffing delicately at everything he saw. And sometimes, as though it were not enough just to smell and to see, he rubbed himself against the edge of a waste basket or the leg of a table.

"What are you doing, you little Sneaker cat?" said the little boy's mother as she came into the room with an armful of letters *"Prowling around,"* said Sneakers, *"Just prowling around."* Just then the wind blew the door open on to the little garden, and it blew the letters out of the little boy's mother's hand, and they went flying all over the floor, and some of them went blowing out into the garden.

"My But I Am Glad This Happened," said Sneakers as he went pouncing after them. "The wind has followed me to town." And he went pouncing around in the little garden while the little boy's mother tried to gather up her spilled letters. "Things don't really change much," thought Sneakers, "even in the city. There are always things to pounce on and places to prowl around." Just then he heard a *sish* in the air. It was a very small noise that the little boy's ears couldn't hear, but Sneakers heard it. It was the flying noise of a bird. And there was the sky! "Oh my," said Sneakers, "The sky has followed me to town, and so have the birds in the sky.

"So many things have followed me to town, I wonder where the green field is with the meadow mouse in it, and the little river with the darting fish. I think I will prowl down this street and look for them. I am sure they will soon be here."

So he and the little boy prowled down the street, and when he got to the end of the block, he peeked around the corner. Where was the green field with the meadow mouse in it? It wasn't there. No green field, no meadow mouse, no shining river, no darting fish. No. Only the fronts of more houses, and no green fields behind them.

So Sneakers prowled along, and he prowled along, and he prowled along the street with the little boy following him. Perhaps around the next corner? He sniffed the air. He smelled dirt and grass, just a tiny smell of it, so tiny that even the little boy's good nose couldn't smell it. But the little cat's nose knew that

49

it was there, and the little cat said, "Good. A field of grass has followed me to town."

And around the next corner, across the street, there was a big field of grass with trees in it. But it was a field such as Sneakers had never seen before. It was filled with benches and children instead of meadow mice. The little boy picked Sneakers up and carried him across the street to show to the other children how his little cat had followed him to town, and how his little cat followed him around wherever he went, like a dog. For Sneakers was the little boy's cat. And so they played in the park under the trees and the falling leaves. The leaves blew around them; and Pounce went Sneakers, Pounce on a yellow leaf, Pounce on a red leaf, Pounce on a little girl's hair ribbon that the wind blew off her head. Pounce. Pounce. Pounce. For Sneakers was a rapscallion cat.

SNEAKERS AND THE EASTER FLOWERS

It was Easter in the city. You could tell it was going to be Easter for a week before it was Easter. Red rose bushes and white hyacinths and lilies appeared suddenly in front of the grocery stores; and the flower stores were so full of flowers that there were potted plants, tulips and daisies, out on the sidewalk. Sneakers thought this was fine when he prowled down the street with the little boy. With a little cat squeal— "Brrrrr-ip"—he arched his back and scratched his side against a flower pot. He even—the little boy looked back just in time to see him—batted a big red tulip with one of his white sneaker paws. "Sneakers! Stop it, you rapscallion cat. Leave those flowers alone."

"Brrrrr-ip," squealed Sneakers and came trotting along. "My favorite flower,—red tulips."

"You weren't even born, Sneakers, last year when the tulips were in bloom."

But Sneakers never thought of anything like that. He wouldn't have believed that there had been a world before he was born, if he had thought about it. Sneakers thought that the world started the day he was born.

51

But the little boy was much older than Sneakers, and he knew better.

They came to a grocery store. The little boy was busy peering in the window at the strawberries and green asparagus and the little red new potatoes. "I certainly do like spring vegetables," he was thinking as he wondered what they would be having for supper when they got home.

He was so busy wondering that he didn't see what Sneakers was doing.

That rapscallion cat was standing on his hind legs with his paws on the edge of a flower pot; and stretching his head way up, he was eating the feathery leaves of the daisy plant.

"Sneakers!" said the little boy. "Get down off of there. Who ever heard of a little black cat eating daisies!"

"Brrrrr-ip," said Sneakers as he jumped down. "My favorite flowers, daisies."

"You weren't even born last year when the daisies were in bloom," said the little boy, who could remember whole fields of white daisies in the country, and buttercups, too.

"But never mind, Sneakers. We'll be going back to the country pretty soon, and I'll show you miles and miles of daisies. And we will go out in a field where you can eat all the daisies you please, if you like to eat daisies."

By this time they had prowled all around the block and were back home again. Sneakers went right into the garden between the iron bars of the fence, but the little boy had to open the iron gate to go in.

THE EASTER SURPRISE

"Tomorrow," said the little boy's Mother at dinner that night, "I have a surprise for you."

"It will be a surprise for Sneakers, too," said the little boy's father. —"A big surprise for Sneakers! We'll hide the surprise in the living room when we hide your Easter eggs."

"Is it more Easter eggs?" asked the little boy.

"No," said his mother, "It's something white."

"And there are two of them," said his father.

"One for me and one for Sneakers?" asked the little boy.

Then his mother and father laughed and laughed. "Not for Sneakers," they said. "NOT FOR SNEAKERS!—But Sneakers will be more surprised than you when he sees them."

"Don't tell him any more," said the cook, "or he'll guess."

So the little boy took his rapscallion cat, and they went up to bed.

"What do you suppose it is, Sneakers?" said the little boy just before he fell asleep.

But fat little Sneakers had already pounced to sleep and was all curled up like a little black fur grapefruit at the foot of the little boy's bed.

SNEAKERS AND THE EASTER BUNNIES

The next morning was Easter. There were a lot of church bells ringing. The sun was streaming in the window, and Sneakers had moved right into the warmest part of the sunshine and was peeking over at the little boy through the narrow slits of his yellow eyes.

"Easter eggs, Sneakers," said the little boy. And he jumped out of bed and was all dressed almost before Sneakers had finished stretching himself. For that was what Sneakers did every morning. He stretched one foot way out, and then another foot. He even stretched his little white toe-pads. And then he shot his back up in the air like a little witch's cat and gave a big yawn to stretch his throat and whiskers.

Then with a little Brrrrr-ip he shot out of the door and down the stairs in front of the little boy.

Sunlight was streaming into the living room. There

were yellow daffodils and flowers in all the vases. And on the desk was a tall green and white Easter lily. A white flower on a long green stem.

And there under the lily plant was a red Easter egg and a yellow Easter egg.

The little boy's mother and father gave him a basket lined with a sort of purple paper grass and told him to put whatever he could find in it.

Behind the sofa pillow he saw something green, and there was a big green goose's egg and a pile of little green jelly-bean eggs. He looked behind all the sofa pillows, but he didn't find any more. He looked under the sofa, and there was something yellow—five little fuzzy yellow cotton chicks.

In the meantime that little rapscallion cat had found a whole nest of little jelly-bean eggs under a chair and was batting them all over the floor. —Another little egg fell off the table. "My, but I'm glad that happened," thought Sneakers, and he batted it across the rug.

Behind some daffodils was a blue egg, and under a hat on the table was a red and a purple one. The little boy was so busy looking for the many colored eggs that he didn't see Sneakers stop and start sniffing the air. He didn't see Sneakers crouch down and start creeping towards the long window curtains with wide staring eyes and padded paws that made no noise.

He just heard his father call in a sharp quick voice —"Sneakers!" Sneakers trembled and stopped moving. And just then out from behind the curtain hopped the smallest white fur bunny with ruby red eyes that the little boy had ever seen. It stretched one long pink ear forward and wiggled its nose.

All this time Sneakers was watching.

Then out from behind the curtain came another little baby bunny and hopped over to the first white bunny. With a kick of its little hind legs and its little pink ears flopping, it came running straight over towards Sneakers.

It ran with little sniffs straight up to Sneakers and rubbed noses.

This was too much for Sneakers. He turned and flew across the room away from that little white bunny, and jumped up on the sofa and sat there switching his tail with round yellow eyes that were bright with anger.

The little bunnies wiggled their noses, kicked up their heels and hopped across the floor looking for something.

"Ho Ho Ho," laughed the little boy's father. "Old Sneakers got fooled that time. The little bunny must have thought Sneakers was a mother rabbit."

"It is a wonder Sneakers didn't pounce on that bunny," said the little boy's mother. "It is very dangerous to let him into the room."

"I was watching him all the time," said the little boy's father. "Poor little Sneakers. He is such a wild rapscallion tiger, and then to have the very thing he was going to catch come running up and rub noses! Little dumb-bunnies!"

The little boy gave them a tulip leaf to nibble, and the little bunnies sat up and nibbled the leaf with little crackling noises of their teeth just like a big bunny. They wiggled their noses as they ate.

The cook brought in some yellow carrots, and the little bunnies just loved that.

And the cook brought something else in. She brought a little catnip pillow for Sneakers, an Easter present. And when Sneakers smelled the catnip pillow, he began to purr and ruffle up his fur; and he curled his little white paws around the catnip pillow and licked and licked it, as happy as a little cat with catnip.

"Now, you Sneakers, you rapscallion cat, don't you come pouncing after my shoelaces any more," said the cook. "And don't you pounce on those little bunnies, either."

"We won't leave them alone together for a while," said the little boy's father. "Sneakers is a mighty hunter, little fat bunnies might be too hard for him to remember not to catch."

So they kept the little bunnies out in the back garden in a little house that the little boy and his father made out of old boxes that they got from the grocery store.

Sneakers went prowling around and prowling around with his fur all fluffed up. He was terribly interested. But Sneakers was such an old pouncer that the little boy and his father were afraid to leave him alone with the bunnies for fear that he would just naturally pounce on the little bunnies and eat them up. For cats are wild animals and mighty hunters when they are brought up in the country, the way Sneakers was. Sneakers had caught his first mouse when he was just a little shaver. And these little white bunnies weren't so much bigger than mice. So the little boy didn't know what Sneakers would do, and he didn't want to take a chance.

But they forgot what an old prowler Sneakers was. And when they weren't looking, Sneakers just prowled out and got into the bunnies' pen. They found him there that afternoon all curled up and sound asleep in one corner of the bunnies' box. And the little bunnies were curled up in another corner of the box close together taking a nap, with their noses wiggling all the time.

"Well," said the little boy's father, "I guess Sneakers likes his white fur company and won't hurt them now that he is used to them. Only I wonder how that little rapscallion cat got in there. I thought I fixed it so that he couldn't."

"Look here," said the little boy.

And there on top of the rabbit house was a loose board that Sneakers had pushed aside with his paw to get into the rabbit house.

"Well," said his father, "let Sneakers play with the little bunnies if he wants to. Tell the cook to always give Sneakers plenty of good things to eat, and I guess the little rabbits will be all right."

Sneakers played with the little bunnies almost as much as the little boy did. Sneakers ate fish and catnip. And the little bunnies ate lettuce and cabbage leaves. And they ate beet tops and carrot tops and carrots that the little boy's friend the grocer gave him every morning to feed them with. He was a very busy little boy in his back garden from then on. Because bunnies eat almost all the time when they aren't scampering about, kicking up their heels, or sleeping, or just sitting around twitching their noses. Then the little boy had to sweep out their pen every day. He was very busy.

And Sneakers that rapscallion cat just went prowling around and prowling around as though he were working too.

THE COUNTRY HAPPENS TO SNEAKERS
AGAIN

Then one day early in the summer or late in the spring—it was hard to tell what it was in the city—something started to happen. The little boy's mother put all his winter clothes away and packed all his summer clothes in a trunk. The cook packed her big feather hat, the little boy's father packed up all his pipes and tobacco and fishing rods and all his clothes. And Sneakers, that rapscallion cat, ran pouncing around and didn't pack a thing. For his little white padded sneakers grew right on his feet, and his little black fur coat grew on his back.

Then one afternoon they all got in the car, and away they went to the country. Sneakers sat on the little boy's lap and peeked out of the window as fast as he could at everything that went by. What was happening now, he wondered. All the world seemed to be racing by. Where were all those telephone posts going, wondered Sneakers. And there went two white houses and a green field in an awful hurry. Where was everything going so fast? But Sneakers never wondered anything for very long, and he didn't like the way he was bouncing up and down, so off he went to sleep where nothing could bother him.

When he woke up, the car had stopped. The little boy was saying, "Wake up, old Sneakers, and see where we are!"

Sneakers blinked his round yellow eyes and stretched himself in a hurry and pounced out of the car right into the green grass of the country. Sniff sniff sniff went Sneakers' black nose. The country! And there were daisy fields and clover fields and shining green fields with yellow buttercups. And there was the old barn where Sneakers went mouse hunting.

Well, here is the country again, thought Sneakers. I wonder where it has been all this time. And there is that big sun just going down over beyond the river with the darting fish. That is just where I left it when I went to the city.

Little Sneakers ran all around, and then he came up and sat on his favorite step on the front porch.

The sun went down in the sky making the clouds all golden red. Little lightning bugs began to flicker in the bushes. And slowly one by one the stars came out in the evening sky.

"My, but I'm glad that happened," thought Sneakers.

THE DEAD BIRD

The bird was dead when the children found it. But it had not been dead for long, it was still warm and its eyes were closed. They felt with their fingers for the quick beat of the bird's heart in its breast. But there was no heart beating. That was how they knew it was dead. And even as they held it, it began to get cold, and the limp bird body grew stiff so they couldn't bend its legs and the head didn't flop when they moved it. That was the way animals got when they had been dead for some time. Cold dead and stone still with no heart beating.

The children were very sorry the bird was dead and could never fly again. But they were glad they had found it, because now they could dig a grave in the woods and bury it. They could have a funeral and sing to it the way grown-up people did when someone died.

So they took it out in the woods and dug a hole in the ground. They put warm sweet ferns in the bottom of the grave, and they wrapped the bird up in grape vine leaves and put it in the ground.

Then they put more ferns on top of it, and little white violets and yellow star flowers. Then they sang a song to it:

> "Oh bird you're dead
> You'll never fly again
> Way up high
> With other birds in the sky
> We sing to you
> Because you're dead
> Feather bird
> And we buried you
> In the ground
> With ferns and flowers
> Because you will never fly
> Again in the sky
> Way up high
> Little dead bird."

Then they cried because their singing was so beautiful and the ferns smelled so sweetly and the bird was dead.

They put dirt over the bird as they sang, and then they put more ferns and flowers and a gray stone on top of the dirt. On the stone they wrote, *Here Lies A Bird That Is Dead*. Around the stone they planted white violet plants, and wild geraniums, only the geraniums faded. And every day until they forgot, they went and sang to their little dead bird and put fresh flowers on his grave.

HOW DO YOU KNOW IT'S SPRING?

How do you know it's Spring?
And how do you know it's Fall?
Suppose your eyes were always shut
And you couldn't see at all.
Could you smell and hear the Spring?
And could you feel the Fall?

THE FIERCE YELLOW PUMPKIN

There was once a small pumpkin in a great big field, a very small pumpkin the size of an apple, just a little green pumpkin. But the sun burned down on the big field, warm on the little pumpkin, and the little pumpkin grew and he grew and he grew under the fierce burning sun. And pretty soon there was a fat little, round little, yellow little pumpkin in a great big field.

Now this fat little round little yellow little pumpkin grew so fat and full of himself that he began to think he was a very fierce vegetable, as fierce as the sun that warmed his fat round sides. "Ho! Ho! Ho!" he would say. "When I grow up and go out into the world Ho! Ho! Ho! I will frighten all the mice and all the vegetables that grow. I'll even frighten the old scarecrow."

For the little pumpkin would dearly have loved to make a fierce ferocious gobble-gobble face like the scarecrow at the far end of the field; but try as he would, his own pumpkin face stayed smooth and yellow and shining.

Then one day the sun did not shine as hot as fire. And black birds, skies full of black birds, began flying over the big field. There was a burning smell of leaves in the air and a crisp tingle that tickled the fat little pumpkin's sides. There were so many birds in the sky that the scarecrow was busy from before daylight until after daylight when it got dark, chasing the birds out of his field. His gobble-gobble face became droopy and dreadful. The wind blew whoo through his hair. He lost one scarecrow eye. For the old scarecrow knew that if there is anything that a black crow is scared of, it is a one-eyed scarecrow. How the little pumpkin wished he were a one-eyed pumpkin! He would scare all the field mice out of the field if he were a one-eyed pumpkin. And then that night and the night after, something began to happen. The first cold frosts came in the night. And the fat little round little yellow little pumpkin woke up one of those mornings and discovered that he was a fiery orange yellow pumpkin. The color of the sun. A fierce burning orange.

Then the children came galloping through the big field and the old one-eyed scarecrow couldn't even make them jump, because they didn't even look at him. They ran right up to the fat little round little orange little pumpkin, and one little girl called out, "Here he is, here is our terrible pumpkin!"

So they cut the pumpkin's heavy stem with a little saw knife; and each taking turns, they carried the pumpkin home, across the field to their house. The little pumpkin liked that. And then with the little saw knife they hollowed him out all empty inside, clean as a whistle, and as sweet smelling as the inside of a pumpkin. They hollowed him all out. Then they cut one big round eye in the side of his face. A big round hole. And the little pumpkin liked that.

"Ho! Ho!" laughed the pumpkin
The fierce yellow pumpkin
"I'm a one-eyed pumpkin
For sure."

Then they cut another big round hole in the other side of his face.

"Ho! Ho!" laughed the pumpkin
The fierce yellow pumpkin
"I'm a fierce yellow pumpkin
For sure."

But that wasn't all. The children cut a sharp shape in the pumpkin for a nose, the shape of a witch's hat. And that wasn't all, either. They took the little saw knife and they sawed zigzag up and zigzag down until the pumpkin had a whole mouth full of sharp zigzag teeth.

Then with a loud Ho! Ho! the little pumpkin laughed a dreadful zigzag laugh across his zigzag teeth.

"Ho Ho Ho
He He He
Mice will run
When they see me."

He was certainly a fierce and ferocious pumpkin with a terrific terrible face.

After a while it was night. There was black darkness all around, inky black darkness.

The children came in with a lighted candle and stuck it inside the pumpkin so that the light shined out his big round eyes and his triangle nose. And the light shined over his zigzag teeth. He was a horrible sight to see. Brrrrr in the dark. He grinned a zigzag grin there in the corner of the room. Grrrr. And the children danced about him singing a song to the terrific terrible pumpkin with the zigzag zigzag grin.

And the little pumpkin was fierce and happy, and he sang:

"Ho Ho Ho
He He He
Mice will run
When they see me!"

And they did.

FALL OF THE YEAR

All the little animals began to grow more fur
All the summer birds began to fly away
The little gray kitten came out of the wind to purr
And the leaves blew away
All in one day
Darkness came before the night
The air grew cold enough to bite
Chrysanthemums were shaggy yellow
The pumpkin became a fierce old fellow
The leaves turned red
The leaves turned brown
They tumbled all over the frosty ground.
The world's on fire in the cold clear air
The world shouts AUTUMN everywhere.

CHRISTMAS EVE

All the children tiptoed downstairs. It was the middle of the night. And night of all nights, it was Christmas. It even looked like Christmas. Great green evergreen branches on the stairs and red berried holly in the halls. Even out the window it looked like Christmas. The quietest night in the world with white snow falling so softly, so quietly. Almost anything could happen on Christmas night.

And something was happening. In the big quiet house where the people were sleeping, the children had gotten up out of their beds. The children had put on their sweaters and slippers and socks and bathrobes and were creeping down the stairs to see their Christmas tree and to see if there would come a man all dressed in red with the kindest face in the world with a sack full of toys and sweet things to eat for children. The children couldn't sleep. They had lain in bed for hours and hours, supposing things, and listening, and pretending. They saw reindeers and sugar plums and angels and stars and wise men.

Then one of the children had said, "Let's all go down and touch the tree and make a wish before we go to sleep." So very quietly in the large cold playroom they had taken their clothes under the covers with them and dressed themselves. Then into the upstairs hall, so quietly, almost without breathing they went, past the door where Mother and Father were sleeping. So quietly through the hall. No sound until the top stair creaked. Then they all stood still, terribly still and listened. No sound but their own thumping hearts. Downstairs it was still warm. The warm smells of Christmas, pine trees and wood smoke and oh wonderful smell of Christmas seals and packages not yet opened. The night before Christmas, Christmas Eve. Quietly listening, listening all over, with eyes and ears and hands and feet they went down into the warm dark pine scented hall.

They came to the livingroom door. They listened. Beyond the window pane, white flakes in the blue night, the snow fell down. They couldn't hear it. A piece of wood creaked in the dying fire.

Then the children went into the room and stood close together on the soft rug in front of the fire. They couldn't speak or move. It was as though a magic had come true. The Christmas tree was all there, trimmed with shiny glints of red and blue and green that flickered in the dying firelight. Silver and gold tinsel hung all over the tree, loads and loads of tinsel, gold tinsel. And in front of the chimney where they could reach out and touch them hung their stockings filled with little white bundles and tangerines and strange shapes. If they reached out their hands they could touch them.

Under the tree were more packages. And there was one big package. They all saw it. It looked like an electric train. It went all around the tree. They all saw it.

No one spoke.   No one moved.

And then suddenly in the night, through the soft snow falling outside, the voices came.   They really came, those voices, so quietly in the night, singing:

> "Holy Night
> Silent Night
> All is calm
> All is bright"

The children ran to the window.

Dark figures were moving outside in the snow.   The dark figures carried a lantern.   They were grown-up people singing.   The children listened.   The sound of the voices seemed to fall with the snow.

> "Sleep in heavenly peace
> Sleep in heavenly peace"

The song stopped.   There was that quietness of snow again.   The grown-up people moved around outside, dark figures against the white snow.   The Christmas Carolers.   They were the Christmas Carolers, grown-up people who went from house to house singing Christmas songs on Christmas Eve.

The children quickly turned toward the stairs. They went up the stairs almost running, only as quietly still as they could.   And they jumped into bed with their clothes on.   Their hearts were pounding.

Then the singing began again:

> "God rest you merry gentlemen
> Let nothing you dismay"

> "Oh Tiding of Comfort and Joy."

BUGS

I like bugs.
Black bugs,
Green bugs,
Bad bugs,
Mean bugs,
Any kind of bug.

A bug in a rug,
A bug in the grass,
A bug on the sidewalk,
A bug in a glass—
I like bugs.

Round bugs,
Shiny bugs,
Fat bugs,
Buggy bugs,
Big bugs,
Lady bugs,
I like bugs.

FISH

I like fish.
Silver fish,
Gold fish,
Black fish,
Old fish,
Young fish,
Fishy fish,
Any kind of fish.

A fish in an ocean,
A fish in a pond,
A fish in a dish
Or the Great Beyond—
I like fish.

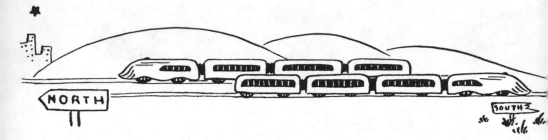

HOW THE LITTLE CITY BOY CHANGED PLACES WITH THE LITTLE COUNTRY BOY FOR A YEAR

There was a little colored boy with brown skin and dark eyes who lived in New York City. He had never been to the country. He saw the vegetables in the markets, he smelled their earthy smells, but he knew the vegetables didn't grow in the market and he wanted to go where the vegetables grew. Summer nights when the older colored people sat on the steps of their houses talking and singing together, he would hear of a country where yellow flowers and green grasses grew, where everyone could have fruits and vegetables growing around their house to pick for their dinners. He heard of strange birds, birds that were not flying from garbage pails with crusts of bread, birds that sang, until it nearly busted your heart wide open to listen to them, as they flew in the warm sunlight over endless fields and bushes. These were not grey birds. There were red birds and blue birds and little yellow birds. There were mockingbirds that copied all the other birds' songs; and a night bird with red eyes that called all night long, "Whip Poor Will, Whip Poor Will." How different that must be from the distant roar of buses and trolleys that never stopped all night long. Sometimes the colored people would speak of the sighing of the pine trees all through the night in the Southland where they had been children. They would speak of the great round moon going down the sky over the cotton fields and over the fields of corn.

There was another little colored boy with brown skin and dark eyes who lived in a pine woods in Fernandina, Georgia. All night long he heard the pine trees sighing around his cabin, and in the morning he was waked up by millions of small birds. That morning, as he was weeding his mother's garden behind the wooden cabin where they lived, two large pelicans flew slowly over his head. He wondered where they came from and where they would go. He wondered what was in the rest of the world away from his little wooden cabin in the pine woods. Did all the world have tall trees with leaves and tall trees with pine needles; and was there always a great ocean not far off where the waves grew as big as houses in a storm? Or was the rest of the world like the pictures of New York City that were down at the post office, with houses that looked like tall narrow hills with holes in them for windows, they were so high? And what did the rest of the world sound like? Old Jack Lacy, who had been to the city once, told him that the city sounded like a terrible storm most of the time, and smelled like gasoline and automobiles and lots of good things to eat cooking. He said the buildings were higher than the trees and that all the people were in a hurry in the daytime. He said that at night there were so many lights on the streets and on the automobiles that it seemed as though hundreds of huge fireflies were flying all around you, making the streets bright as day.

The little boy thought it would be wonderful to see a big city, as he weeded his mother's garden. He thought it would be wonderful to hear the roar of a big city, and smell a big city. So much food cooking for so many people. The little boy wiggled his nose to the smoke from his own cabin, to the smell of bacon and greens cooking on his mother's stove. What did they eat for lunch in New York City? The pine trees whispered over his head. All about him there was a warm sharp smell of pine in the summer air.

What did a big city sound like when the wind blew at night?

Then one day his mother got a letter. They heard the Mail Man's mule coming down the road, clop clop whoa. And the mail man got off and waited for the little boy's mother to open her letter. Then he helped her read the letter, because the little boy's mother could only read a few words. She had been so busy all her days growing green vegetables and taking care of her little boy, she hadn't had a chance to learn to read.

"You say this letter says that my little boy can go to New York City and go to school this year if I will let my sister's little boy from New York City come down here and learn to hoe corn and weed the potato patch? What do you think about that, Mail Man?"

"I think you better let your little boy go and see New York City for a year and learn to read and write up there in those big schools," said the Mail Man.

So one day the little country boy got on a train with a package of sandwiches to eat, kissed his mother goodbye, and rode away on the train to New York City, off across the cotton fields and through the pine trees, going **north.**

That same day the little boy in New York City got on the train in a big white marble station. He had on a brand new suit, and he had fifteen dimes in his pocket to buy sandwiches with. He kissed his mother goodbye and rode away in his brand new suit, through tunnels and over bridges, going south.

The little boy going south looked out the window. He saw big factories. He saw big towns with many houses where many people lived. He saw roads and automobiles. And every once in a while he saw the country with the green grass growing all around, and horses and cows in the fields. He saw some trees against the sky on a hill.

The other little boy going north from Fernandina looked out the window. He saw long empty stretches of flat cotton fields. He went through swamps where long grey moss hung from the trees like old men's beards. He went through corn fields where the corn was cut and stacked in piles. He went through cotton fields where the round soft cotton blossoms were just bursting white on the little green cotton plants.

Both little colored boys had eyes as big as saucers. They had never been away from home before. And they had never seen so much all in one day. It was only when the little boy from New York heard a man coming through the train calling, "Ice cream, ham sandwich," that he remembered the shiny new dimes his mother had given to him. So the little boy bought two ice cream bricks all for himself.

It was only when the little boy from Fernandina saw a man milking a cow in a field that he remembered the package of good sandwiches and pecan pralines his mother had packed for him.

The little boys traveled two days and a night. They saw all the land between New York and Fernandina except when it was too dark to see. They saw mountains and rivers and cities and the ocean. They saw too many things to tell about all at once. They even saw each other's train go rushing by like a house on fire through the dark.

And when the little colored boy from Fernandina got to New York and went to bed that night on the tenth floor of a big tall house, he was very sleepy. He could look from his window and see red and green lights winking on and off way up the big city street. But the little boy was too sleepy to see much that first night. He closed his big eyes, and his little brown ears listened only to the first taxicab blow its horn. He didn't hear the second time it blew. The little boy was sound asleep. He might have been anywhere, North or South, for all he knew when he was asleep.

And when the little colored boy from New York City got to Fernandina, Georgia, his aunt put him right to bed after a great big hot supper. And the little

80

colored boy from New York City heard one bird call way down the road, *Whip Poor Will, Whip Poor Will.* He heard the pine trees sighing and singing a soft sleepy song outside his window. And then quick as the chirp of one cricket, the little boy was asleep. Then the little boy was so sound asleep he might have been anywhere, North or South, for all he knew when he was asleep.

But the next day each little boy woke up in a brand new world. And for a whole year, autumn, winter, spring, and summer, until the little boy in the South went home to New York and the little boy in the North went home to Fernandina, Georgia, the two little boys saw and heard and smelled and felt many things they had never known before. And only the little city children know some of these things, and only the little country children know some of these things.

THE SONGS THAT ARE SUNG
TO AN AEROPLANE

There was once
A brave little aeroplane
Who flew through the wind
And the snow and the rain.
And he heard their songs
Again and again,
The songs that are sung
To an aeroplane.

I am the rain
      the rain
           the rain
I get you wet
Little Aeroplane

I am the snow
      the snow
           the snow
I make you cold
When the cold winds blow

I am the wind
    the wind
        the wind
I blow the snow
I blow the rain
    And I blow *you*
        Little Aeroplane

Snow rain wind snow
  Will always be
  Wherever you go
Rain snow wind rain
  Will always be,
  Little Aeroplane.

THE RAT THAT SAID BOO TO THE CAT

Once there was a rat. And if there was anything that he did not like, it was cats. He jumped when he saw a cat. And he did NOT like them.

He lived in the barn under the cement near an old dump heap where the farmer threw all the old rotten vegetables that he didn't want. It was a continual feast for the rat, because he loved rotten vegetables better than ice cream or fudge or chicken soup.

Now this might have been a very pleasant life that the rat was living. But there was one big bother in his life. The Cat. The cat that lived in the stable loved to eat fat rats; so that whenever the rat was nibbling a ripe rotten pumpkin, he had to keep one eye moving around to make sure that the cat was not creeping up on him. For he was a nice fat rat, the kind any cat would find simply delicious. And he knew it. So he always rolled his eyes round and round as he ate.

One day as he was gnawing through a tough green cucumber with his long sharp teeth, his rolling eyes

84

saw a black pointed ear wiggle just a little bit over near the barn door. It was the cat. The black surreptitious slinking cat peeking over the edge of a bucket of water. But the rat kept right on gnawing faster and faster, because he didn't want the cat to know that he had seen him. It was safer to keep on eating and then stroll away to some nice safe hole in the ground where the cat couldn't follow. But there would be no dessert to-day. In fact . . . it was time not to stroll but to dart away. Zip! The rat was off as fast as his claws could scratch up the ground.

And ZIP, the cat was after him, going about thirty miles an hour. The only trouble was that the cat was between the rat and the barn, so that the rat had to run around a bit before he could get back to his hole under the cement.

So ZIP he ran here and ZIP he ran there, and ZIP the cat came running after him. Zip around a cabbage,

Zip across a water trough

Zip through the garden

Zip zip zip! and the cat

came running after him.

Finally the little rat was so fat and so tired that he knew that he could only run about two more minutes. What must he do? He thought as he ran. One minute was gone. He thought very quickly now. Another minute was almost gone when the rat turned and stopped, and rolling his eyes at the galloping cat, said "Boo."

85

The cat was so surprised that he stopped dead in his tracks. He stared at the rat with his eyes wide open.

"Silly old cat, this is what I'm going to do. I'm going to leap upon your back and start to eat you."

The old cat blinked his eyes. And at the first blink the rat was away and scooting toward the hole under the cement. ZIP. He was gone.

The cat flew to the hole and sniffed and sniffed. But it was too late. The little fat rat was safe, and just curling up for his evening nap.

And this is what the rat dreamed that night when the wind was howling outside and the horses were stomping in their stalls.

> There was a little rat
> Upon a little cat.
> He ate the little cat
> And he got fat.

And this is what the cat dreamed that night when the wind was howling outside and the horses were stomping in their stalls.

> There was a little cat
> Upon a little rat.
> He ate the little rat
> And he got fat.

THE CHILDREN'S CLOCK

Once upon a time there was a clock—Tick tock tick tock, a most ridiculous clock. Summer and winter it never stopped, tick tock ten o'clock tick tock eleven o'clock tick tock tick tock, a most ridiculous clock.

It was a very good clock for the people who could read the numbers on it and knew what the numbers meant. But for children it was no good, because they didn't know what numbers meant. It was the most ridiculous clock to them, the tick was the same as the tock and what was the difference between two and ten o'clock?

But one day there were some children who said, We will make a clock for ourselves that will tell us what we want to know. So they began with a big circle—for the day. They asked where on the clock was seven o'clock. For at seven o'clock they woke up and got up from their beds, and they would paint a picture of a bed at seven o'clock. They would paint a picture that looked

87

like the early morning, with the sun showing through a window, on the spot where it said seven o'clock. Then, said the children, there is breakfast time. What place on the clock says breakfast time? And the grown-ups showed them a place between seven and eight o'clock that was breakfast time. They moved the short hand there by moving the long hand half way around the clock. And on that spot where the short hand pointed to between seven and eight, they drew a picture of a glass of orange juice, and an egg, and a dish of cereal, on a breakfast table.

Then we must draw a picture of the Nursery School, they said. And they drew a picture on the place where the grown-ups showed them that it said nine o'clock. It was the picture of their school, with children in it and smoke coming out of the chimney. And after that they painted a picture of blocks and books and paintings and a shootty-shoot. And then they put a picture of a glass of tomato juice where the grown-ups showed them the place on the clock that said half past ten o'clock. Then at noon they painted their lunch on the spot that said twelve o'clock, right at the tip top of the clock. And so they went right through their day on the clock until they came back to seven o'clock at night, when they put another window by the bed, with stars showing through to show that it was night. For they got up at seven o'clock in the morning with the sun shining in their window, and they went to bed at night with the moon and the stars shining in their window.

Then the grown-ups showed them how the short

hand of the clock went all around the face of the clock while they were asleep at night. It went from seven o'clock at night all the way around to seven o'clock in the morning, and took just as long to get around at night as it took in the day. That was how long the night was—as long as it took the short hand of the clock to get from the picture of the bed back to the picture of the bed. Only the children were asleep all this time and never knew. But the long hand had to go around the face of the clock twelve times during the night. It had to go all the way around the face of the clock, from the top of the clock back to the top of the clock once every hour. It was a very busy hand.

And that was how the children made their own clock, a clock that they could read. Tick Tock Tick Tock, a most pictorial punctual clock! Lunch o'clock and play o'clock and bed o'clock to the same tick tock as the most ridiculous grown-up clock.

But it was not very long, not even a year, before the children could read the numbers on every clock themselves and know what the numbers meant.

LITTLE LOST KITTEN

Little lost kitten
Lost in the rain
I look for you
Over and over again

THE LITTLE GIRL'S MEDICINE

Once upon a time there was a little girl who lived way out in the country on a big tobacco farm. She had no brothers and sisters. She had no one to play with, this poor little girl, and she had to play all by herself. She played all by herself year after year and talked to her parents when they ate their meals.

One day, after a while, the little girl became sick. No one knew what was the matter. It was in late August, when they hitched up the four black mules and hauled the tobacco plants away to the big drying barns. But the little girl didn't want to go with them and drive the four big mules. She just sat.

That night there was peach ice cream for dinner, but the little girl didn't want any. She just sat. When it was time to go to bed, she didn't even care.

"Oh Dear," said her mother to her father, "our little girl is sick. She loves to drive the four black mules when they haul the tobacco from the fields to the barns, and yet she wouldn't go. She just sat. And she loves peach ice cream, but she wouldn't eat it to-night. She just sat. And she didn't even want to stay up and play when it was time to go to bed. Our little girl must be sick."

So they took the little girl to the doctor in the big city.

The little girl's mother said to the doctor in the big city, "Doctor, my little girl is very sick."

"What is the matter with your little girl?" asked the doctor. "Has she a sore throat?"

And the little girl's mother said, "Doctor, my little girl doesn't want to drive the mules with the tobacco loads any more, and she doesn't like peach ice cream any more, and she doesn't care whether it is bed time or whether it isn't bed time. So I fear that she must be a very sick little girl."

"What!" said the doctor, "Doesn't like peach ice cream! This is serious! Little girl, stick out your tongue."

So the little girl stuck out her tongue, and the doctor looked at it very carefully. "It is a perfectly good tongue that you have in your head, little girl," said the doctor. "Let me see your throat, little girl. Say Ahhhhhhhhh."

So the little girl leaned her head way back, way back, and opened her mouth so wide that she looked like a baby robin asking for food. The doctor took a flashlight and peered down into the little girl's throat. "Say Ahhhhhhhh," he said.

Then he said, "Little girl, let me feel your pulse."

So he held the little girl's wrist in his hand, and with his fingers he listened very carefully, counting the beats of the little girl's heart that he could feel in the veins of her wrist. "It's a perfectly good heart that you have in you, little girl; but if you don't like to play any more and don't like peach ice cream any more, you are very sick. It would be a pity if your brothers and sisters caught what is wrong with you."

"But I have no brothers and sisters," said the little girl.

"But your cousins and friends might catch it," said the doctor.

"Only I haven't any cousins; and I haven't any friends," said the little girl.

"Then the small animals on the place might catch it," said the doctor.

"There aren't even any small animals," said the little girl, "Not even a little pig. Just four big old black mules that kick every time anyone goes near them."

"Well," said the doctor, "this is serious. I will have to prescribe something to make you well."

The doctor sat there for a long time nodding his head, while the little girl and her mother waited. Then he got up and walked around the room three times. Then he opened a book and read three pages of it. Then he coughed three times and he said,

"Little girl, I have just the thing that will make you well." So he took out his pencil and wrote it down on a piece of paper, folded it, and handed it to the little girl's mother.

"If you will have this prescription filled," he said to the little girl's mother, "and give it to your little girl right away, I am sure that she will get well."

So the little girl's mother folded up the prescription in her purse without looking at it, thanked the doctor, and went out of his office with the little girl.

"We will go right to the drug store first thing," said the little girl's mother, "and have this prescription filled before lunch." So they went into the drug store next door, and the little girl's mother handed the prescription to the druggist, still folded up as the doctor had given it to her.

The druggist was an old man, and he unfolded it slowly.

"Hmmmp," he said. Then he said it again. "Hmmmmp!"

"Do you expect me to fill this prescription?"

"Why, of course," said the little girl's mother. "Haven't you got that kind of medicine?"

Then the druggist, old as he was, just threw back his head and hollered with laughter. "Do you know what this prescription says?" he asked.

The little girl's mother took the prescription and read it. And this is what the prescription said—

One fat puppy dog
to be given to the little girl
immediately
signed
Doctor Wwwwwwwww.

"I have filled prescriptions for thirty years," laughed the druggist, "but never a prescription for a

puppy dog. —But wait!" he said. "Wait a minute.
—I—think that I can fill this prescription after all.
Right across the street. Will you come with me?"
he said.

So the little girl and her mother followed the druggist, still chortling and laughing to himself, out the
door and across the street to a house that had a back
yard.

The little girl and her mother followed him right
into the back yard, and there in a box was one furry
little puppy dog all by himself.

"This is the last one left," said the druggist. "They
belong to my sister, and she is giving them away. So
if the doctor says the little girl needs a puppy, this is
how we can fill the prescription for her."

"My puppy?" asked the little girl. "All mine?"

"Yes," said the druggist. "That is your puppy if
you want him, and you can take him right along home
with you this minute."

The little puppy wiggled and jumped around the
little girl as if he was just as glad as she was that they
would have each other to play with. He had been
sitting all by himself in that empty box, just one little
puppy all by himself for two long days. He hadn't
even eaten the milk that was still in his saucer.

So the little girl took her puppy right home with
her. They got back just as the big wagon with the four
black mules was going out of the gate. The little girl's
father was driving.

"Hey, little girl," he called, "do you want to go
out after the last load with me?"

"Indeed I do!" said the little girl. "And look what I am going to bring with me!"

She jumped out of the car with the puppy under her arm and climbed up on the wagon beside her father.

"For goodness sakes!" he said. "What in the world have you got there?"

"This," said the little girl, "is my medicine, and I feel much better already."

"Well, come here, Medicine," said the little girl's father. "Are you going to learn to be a good tobacco farmer like me and the little girl?"

Little fat Medicine (for that was the puppy's name from then on) wiggled right up in her father's arms and licked him on the nose, and they all drove along on the wagon together behind the four black mules. They hauled the last load of tobacco on to the wagon and hauled it away to the big tobacco drying barns and hung it up on the racks to dry. It was hard hot work. And then they went home to supper.

And what do you think they had for dessert, and the fat little puppy had a spoonful of it, too? Peach ice cream.

And that night when it was time to go to bed, up the steps scampered the little girl, and up the steps scampered the little puppy. And they both scampered right into the little girl's room. And together that night the little girl and her Medicine went right off to sleep, all curled up in their warm little beds in the same room.

SLEEPY

STORIES

LITTLE DONKEY CLOSE YOUR EYES

Little Donkey on the hill
Standing there so very still
Making faces at the skies
Little Donkey close your eyes.

Little Monkey in the tree
Swinging there so merrily
Throwing cocoanuts at the skies
Little Monkey close your eyes.

Silly Sheep that slowly crop
Night has come and you must stop
Chewing grass beneath the skies
Silly Sheep now close your eyes.

Little Pig that squeals about
Make no noises with your snout
No more squealing to the skies
Little Pig now close your eyes.

Wild young birds that sweetly sing
Curve your heads beneath your wing
Dark night covers all the skies
Wild young birds now close your eyes.

Old black cat down in the barn
Keeping five small kittens warm
Let the wind blow in the skies
Dear old black cat close your eyes.

Little child all tucked in bed
Looking such a sleepy head
Stars are quiet in the skies
Little child now close your eyes.

THE POLITE LITTLE POLAR BEAR

Once there was a polite little polar bear who lived in the wide icy regions of the Far North. He lived in a cave of ice in the frozen snow.

This little polar bear had a delightful manner with the fish he ate. "Please, little fish, may I eat you up?" he would say; and the fish were so surprised at such lovely manners in a polar bear that they were frozen with surprise, and the polite little polar bear fished them out from under the ice with one curving swoop of his long fur paw. Then off he loped across the ice on his fur-soled feet, growling happily to himself with his belly full of fish.

One day when the little polar bear was out walking, he met an angry old seal and three rude walruses.

"Bah to you!" said the angry old seal.

"Boo to you!" said the three rude walruses.

But the little polar bear, the polite little polar bear, said, "How very delighted I am to meet three rude walruses and an angry old seal all in one morning!"

"Bah to you, Little Polar Bear," said the angry old seal.

"Boo to you," said the three rude walruses and shuffled along on their way across the frozen ice to look for fish.

"Unfortunately, Old Seal," growled the polite little polar bear, "I am not very hungry today, so I regret that I will not be able to eat you this minute. But I look forward very much to meeting you again." And the little polar bear went on his way across the frozen ice.

It was such a beautiful icy summer's day, the polite little polar bear felt like a good fifty-mile swim before supper. So when he got to the edge of the great green waters, he slipped from the ice in a walloping dive and swam away off across the icy sea. He rolled through a floating sea meadow of tiny green water plants that grow in the arctic sea, and he batted at some sea butter-flies, the kind whales eat. Then he swam on and on through the summer sea, past big ice cakes all white and shining.

He swam and he swam the way polar bears swim miles and miles in the arctic sea for the fun of it; and then suddenly the little polar bear was sleepy, and he wanted to take a nap. But where to take it? He was many miles from the flat fields of ice he had come from, and he was in a hurry to get to sleep. So he turned around; and with just his nose out of the water, he swam as fast as he could back towards the ice flats and his own icy cave. He was in an awful hurry to get to sleep.

All of a sudden there was a very small iceberg,

just a baby iceberg, in front of him. It was too steep to climb up on; and the little polar bear was in such a hurry, he didn't feel like swimming around it. The little iceberg went too deep down into the water for him to swim under it. So he said,

"Please, Little Iceberg, get out of my way. If you will be so kind, get out of my way."

But the little baby iceberg just floated right where it was in the arctic sea. Right in the polite little polar bear's way.

"Please, Little Iceberg, the water is cold, and I'm terribly sleepy, and I'm not very old. And as I said before, this water is cold."

But the little baby iceberg just floated right where it was in the arctic sea. Right in the polite little polar bear's way.

"Little Baby Iceberg, if I weren't so polite, I would duck you in the water where you couldn't see the light. Oh, bother!" said the polar bear, "Why am I so polite?"

But the little iceberg stayed right where it was in the arctic sea. All this time the little polar bear was getting sleepier and sleepier, so he just swam right around that silly little iceberg; and there on the other side was the flat ice and a nice fat seal sound asleep for his supper. So he politely ate the seal without even waking it up. He ate sixty pounds of seal before he was full, and then he fell asleep under the midnight sun, looking like a fat little lump of white snow on the rest of the white snow, in the wide icy regions of the Far North.

LITTLE BROWN TUG

With a puff and a chug
And away through the foam
A little brown tug
Was heading for home

He passed a big steamer
Headed out toward the sky
And he blew all his whistles
To see it go by

But with puff and a chug
And a splash through the foam
The little brown tug
Kept heading for home.

THE WONDERFUL KITTEN

Once there were four little kittens, a little fur pile of kittens. And they lived on a white wooly sheepskin rug in the clothes closet. When they were born they were as small as a mouse and as big as a bird. They all had whiskers and claws and noses and tiny round ears and tails. But their little eyes were closed tight shut for two weeks, and they didn't have any teeth. All they could do was to kick with their paws in the air and squeak.

Their mother thought they were so beautiful that the minute they were born she began to purr. She purred them a cat song as they lay by her side.

> Purr Purr
> My cat whiskered mouse
> Come close to my sides
> For this is your house
> Purr Purr
> My Kitten—O—Mouse

Fluff Ball Angel, for that was the mother cat's name, loved her little fur kittens. She loved them with a long steady purr.

Purrrrrrrrrrrrrrrrrrrr. Purrrrrrrrrrrrrrrrrrrrr. And her eyes were bright and shiny when she purred. She curled up her paws and waved them in the air.

For they were four beautiful round fur kittens in a little fur pile. One little kitten was white as the

snow, and one little kitten was grey. One little kitten
was black as the night, and one little kitten had yellow
stripes on his black coat like a wee baby tiger. They
crawled around their mother's sides for a long time.
Then one day after they had had their little blue eyes
open for a week, one of them said, "Peep, Peep. What
a wonder-full kitten I am. I can Yawn some, Sneeze
some, Purr some, Lick some, See some, Hear some, and
CRAWL. I'm a wonderful cat the size of a rat and
I think I will crawl away."

So he waved his four black paws in the air, because
he was on his back when he thought about crawling
away. But he didn't get anywhere by waving his paws
in the air. He stayed in the very same spot. So then
he wiggled and wriggled until he got his fat little
stomach to roll over. And there he was on his legs.

Hic-^{up}.

"Fiddlesticks," said the little Kitten. "What's
that?" And he opened his eyes, his brand new eyes,
and looked all about.

Hic

There it went again!

Hic

He looked at all his brothers and sisters. But there
they were all curled up sound asleep. What could that
noise be?

Hic-^{up} —This time the little kitten shook all over
when the noise came.

"Why it's me!" said the little kitten. "What a wonderful kitten I am.—I can Yawn some, Sneeze some,

Purr some, Lick some, See some, Hear some, Crawl some, and HIC-UP. I'm a wonderful cat the size of a rat and I think I will crawl away." And this time, on his little shaky legs with his tail in the air, he began to crawl away. He spread his toes and put one foot forward. Then he spread his toes and put the other foot forward. He crawled all the way across the sheepskin and out the closet door. There was the little black kitten in the hall. What a big vast hall it was. The little kitten stretched his neck in every direction and looked way out across the gray hall rug.

Zzzzzz

Bzzzzz —along came flying a big black fly.

"Whufff," said the little black kitten—"What is that?" And the hair stood up on him till he looked like an angry black pom-pom.

Zzzzz Zzzzzzzzzzzzzzzz

The little kitten arched his back and stood on his shaky legs and——Spt. He spit.

Then the zzzzzzz got softer and when the little kitten finally saw what it was with his brand new eyes, the fly was just a little buzzing spot up in the air.

"Fiddlesticks," said the kitten. "What a tiny little black spot. And what a wonderful kitten I am. I can Yawn some, Sneeze some, Purr some, Lick some, See some, Hear some, Crawl some, Hic-up and SPIT. And I'm not afraid of anything."

And on he crawled into the middle of the hall, way out across the rug all by himself.

But before long, because he was a very little kitten,

and he couldn't think much better than he could crawl, the little black kitten couldn't remember where he was or where he was going. And his brand new eyes couldn't see away back across the rug as far as the white sheepskin inside the closet door. The little kitten was lost in the middle of the great gray rug. Lost in the great vast hall. And the little kitten was cold without the other warm fur kittens. And his shaky little legs, his brand new legs, shook so that he fell over on his side.

"Oh dear," cried the little kitten. "I don't like this." And then he remembered that he could squeal and squeak.

"Squeeeeeeeee Squeeeeeeeee Squeeeee" went the brand new kitten. "I'm a little lost kitten and I don't know where I am."

He squealed so loud that his mother, Fluff Ball Angel, heard him. Fluff Ball Angel had been away all this time on Fluff Ball Angel business in the next room. But when she heard her little black kitten squealing, she came running. Brrrrrip———— Mmmrrrrrrrrip———— ————She ran right up to her little black kitten on the gray rug in the great vast hall and she licked his face with her tongue and she rolled him over with her paw and licked him until he was all warm and happy and didn't squeal any more. He was with his mother so he didn't care where he was. He just lay on his back and purred to himself. And he thought to himself, What a Wonderful kitten I am. I can Yawn some, Sneeze some, Purr some, Lick some, See some, Hear some, Crawl some, Hic-up,

Spit, and SQUEAL. What a WONDERFUL kitten
I am. And now I want to go home.

So Fluff Ball Angel picked him up by the loose
skin on the back of his neck. She picked him up very
gently and holding her head very high so she wouldn't
drag him on the floor, she carried him across the wide
gray rug, right through the closet door and she dropped
him right in the pile with his brothers and sisters.
Then she lay down by her little pile of kittens. And
she scrubbed the little kitten that was white as snow,
and she scrubbed her kitten that was gray, and she
scrubbed her kitten that looked like a tiger, and she
scrubbed the little black kitten who had run away.
She scrubbed them with her tongue. Then she curled
herself around them and purred them a cat song.

> Purr Purr
> My cat whiskered mouse
> Come close to my sides
> For this is your house
> Purr Purr
> My kitten—O—mouse.

Then all the little kittens felt full and sleepy. And
the little white kitten purred himself to sleep and the
little gray kitten purred himself to sleep and the little
tiger cat purred himself to sleep. And the little black
kitten just curled in a little black ball and rolled right
off to sleep before he could remember all the wonderful
things he could do. He just went to sleep.

FISH SONG

Oh the lobster and the fish
And the fish and the whale
You can't catch a fish
With an old tin pail
And you can't catch a lobster
With a hook and a line
And you can't catch a whale at all.

Catch a lobster in a pot
And a fish on a line
Fish in the nets
When the weather is fine
But if ever you try to catch a whale
He will knock you down flat
With a flip of his tail.

THE BOYS WHO FLEW AWAY

A Dream

Two little boys one summer night
Flew out of the window
And out of sight
One summer night.

They flew away to a cloudy sky
Above the world
Away up high
Where huge clouds go sailing by
Among the stars
Where no birds fly.

And there on a cloud the boys would lie
Sailing all over the windy sky
Until they woke up to a summer day
And found they had dreamed the night away.

WHEN I SHUT MY EYES

When I shut my eyes at night
The world is dark
There is no light
I hear the sound of horses' feet
Clop clop clopping down the street
Far away in the dark
I hear a distant dog bark
I hear the low boat whistles moan
They are going far from home
I hear the sound of ladies' feet
Tap tap tapping down the street
Then I hear the quiet boom
Of something dropping in a room
And then I dream things in my head
Until I fall asleep in bed.

THE WILD BLACK CROWS

A Circular Song

The wild black crows flew over the woods and flew far away. They flew far away and they never came back any more.

And the woods were so quiet when the crows were gone that the nuts falling from the treetops made the squirrels jump and scamper away. Just the leaves falling in the deep smelling woods, and the leaves rotting and the small birds singing, and no angry scream of a crow.

Where had they gone, the wild black crows, to leave the woods so still? Nobody knows until this day, any more than that they went away and never came back any more.

And the woods were so quiet when the crows were gone. . . .*

. . .

---

*Repeat the second and third paragraph until a child goes to sleep, over and over again as though the story went on and on and never ended, until sleep.

THE LITTLE BLACK CAT WHO WENT
TO MATTITUCK

There was a little black cat who wanted to run away. So he said, "I think I will go to Mattituck." And down the road he went. Trot trot trot on his way to Mattituck. Trot trot trot on his little padded paws. Trot trot trot down the black tar road without a sound.

Now this little black cat who wanted to run away lived out in the country and Mattituck was the name of the nearest town. This little cat had never been to any town before, not even to the nearest town. He had just lived all his life on a potato farm in the country. All his life he had looked at long flat stretches of potato fields and blue sky and white farm houses.

It was a dark night when the little cat ran away. There was no light on the road and the bushes at the side of the road were even darker. The little cat ran on down the black tar road farther and farther away from home towards Mattituck. Pretty soon he came to a part of the road where he could see little flickering lights in the bushes.

"Whiff," said the little cat, and he stopped where he was and the hairs stood up all over him. "What, Oh What is that?" He blinked and he blinked at the flickering lights in the bushes. The lights moved on and off. One minute they were here and one minute they were there. "Whiff," said the little cat on his way to Mattituck. "Can this be the town with all the flicker-

ing lights?" and he trotted over to the bushes to see.
But when he got in the bushes what did he see?—A lot
of little bugs drifting through the grasses flashing little
lights on and off.—Lightning bugs.

"This is certainly not a town," said the little cat and
he trotted on his way to Mattituck, down the black tar
road. Trot trot he went on his little padded paws without a sound.

"Whoo Wh^{oo}," said a wide eyed owl from the top
of a tree.

"Who Who^{oo} Who are You?"
"I am a little black cat and I'm running away down
the black tar road to Mattituck."
"Better go back Better go back Better go back,"
chirped the crickets from the ditches at the side of the
road.

"Whoo Who^{oo}" said the wide eyed owl from the
top of a tree.

But the little black cat didn't pay any attention to
any of them. He was running away and he was going
to Mattituck, and so that was what he did. Way
down the road through the darkness on his little
padded paws.

Pretty soon he came to a lot of big dark square
shapes that were houses with no lights on.

"Hmmp," said the little black cat. "I must be
getting to Mattituck." And with that he began to purr.
He purred like a little thunder bug as he padded along
through the sleeping town. His eyes grew rounder
and larger as he looked all around and up and down

the road. So this was a town, a sleeping town. There were long rows of houses up and down the road. The doors of all the houses were closed, but the windows were open. All the lights were out.

"Hmmp," said the little black cat. "I wonder who lives in that little white house." So he trotted up the front path to the house. The front door was closed, so the little cat climbed up a tree near the house and looked in a window on the second floor. At first the room seemed dark and he couldn't see very much. Even with his little cat eyes that saw at night, it was hard to see at first. Then he saw a little girl with red hair sound asleep in bed.

"Hmmp," said the little cat who went to Mattituck. "Hmmp! NO PUSSYCATS. Just a little girl with red hair sound asleep lives here. Not much for me to see." Then Scratch Scratch the little black cat climbed down the tree and went away from the little red haired girl's house.

And the little girl slept soundly in the room by herself and never knew that the little cat who went to Mattituck had seen her.

The little cat trotted up the road on his little padded paws without a sound. Pretty soon he came to a very big house. He couldn't see what color the house was in the dark, but it was a great big house with three chimneys and a porch on every side of it.

"What a fine big house," thought the little cat. "There must be a pussycat lives in that." So scritch scritch scratch he scrambled up a tree that grew in front of an open window.

The little black cat opened his eyes very wide and very round and he peered through the darkness inside the window. At first he could just see a long lump under the bed clothes. It wasn't as long as the whole bed, and it wasn't as short as half of the bed. Beside the bed was a little silver toy airplane and over in one corner of the room was an electric train.

"Hmmp," said the little black cat who went to Mattituck. "No PUSSYCATS. That lump in the bed must be a little boy with his head almost under the covers."

Then SCRATCH SCRATCH the little black cat backed down the tree and trotted on up the road.

And the little boy sound asleep in the big house never knew that the little cat who went to Mattituck had seen him.

Pretty soon the little black cat came to a new part of the town. All the houses had big glass windows across the front of them. And in the windows were all sorts of things. In the windows the little black cat could see wheelbarrows and shovels and clocks and dresses and candy and boxes and vegetables and baby carriages.

"Hmmp" said the little black cat who went to Mattituck. "No PUSSYCATS. There are no pussycats in the stores of Mattituck. No pussycats and I am getting sleepy. But I must climb one more tree and look in one more window before I go home and go to sleep."

So he went up to the biggest house in town and scritch scritch scratch he scrambled right up a little sycamore tree as high as the second floor. And then he looked into the biggest window in the house.

And this is what he saw——Two little boys and one little girl in three little beds. He saw some dolls and fire engines in one corner of the room. And on one of the little boy's beds was a shaggy airdale dog. The little cat could see that the airdale dog was sound asleep with his eyes closed. On a table in the room was a big glass bowl of gold fish that swam round and round without a sound. Round and round and round and round. And then, there in a basket by the little girl's bed was an old mother cat and six little pussycats.

"Hmmp," said the little black cat. "I'm glad I saw that. Not one but six little pussycats." And he looked and he looked and he looked at them. Six little kittens who would grow up and run around and play.

But just then the old dog shot his legs out straight in front of him and curled up his back and yawned, and stretched—Grryow.

"For goodness sakes," said the little cat who went to Mattituck, "I must be going."

And Scritch Scratch Scritch Scratch the little black cat backed down the tree. And when he got to the ground he trotted off down the road through the sleeping town towards home.

So Trot Trot Trot back up the black tar road on his little padded paws went the little black cat, pad pad pad without a sound. And he got back to his potato farm just in time to get to sleep before it was time to wake up. And that was how the little black cat ran away and went to Mattituck.

FOUR FISHING BOATS

Four little boats
   Late in the day
Hoisted their sails
   And sailed away
Over the ocean
   And out toward the sky
Four little boats went sailing by.

    They sailed all night
    In the dark night light
    Over high black waves
    Of tremendous height
    They sailed all night.

Four little boats
   Early next day
Furled their sails
   In a quiet bay
Then they waited for fish
   To run that way
And the four little boats fished all day.

THE PALE BLUE FLOWER

All the butterflies in the world were flying in the air, up in the air across the sky. They were looking for one pale small flower that was blue, the pale blue flower that was hard to find. They flew over the daisy fields, the green and white fields. They flew over the wheat fields where the scarlet poppies grew, and the deep blue cornflowers, green and red and blue. They flew over the people's gardens, over the wild yellow jonquils bent in the wind, and the purple hyacinths, purple as the night. They flew over green lawns where sudden little crocuses appeared in the grass, yellow and white and lavender, like colored easter eggs. They flew all over the world in the spring looking for the pale blue flower that was hard to find.

They flew, wings flashing in the sunlight. And then they came to where the children were picking wild strawberries in the woods. The children had little baskets made of sticks, and as they leaned over to pick the red strawberries they smelled the wild sharp smell and the warm quiet smell of new grasses and the dark smell of the earth. They heard little buzzing sounds, sounds of black insects in the grass, and they saw the shadows of butterflies flying along the ground. All around, the sun was warm, golden warm on the children's backs.

Then almost by accident the little boy found the small blue flower, the pale blue flower that was hard to find. Only he didn't know it was hard to find. He just found it. He saw it there in the grass and he called to the other children, "Look. It is a small blue flower that I have never seen before." And the other children came running to see. "Let's pick it," said one of the children, but the little boy said, "No. Let's leave it here to grow. There are not many pale blue flowers like this in the world."

So they left the flower and went on picking the red strawberries. And all the butterflies in the world flew away back to the other flowers where they got their honey. They had seen the small blue flower that is hard to find. And the small blue flower is still growing in the grasses where children sometimes find it by accident, suddenly. A pale blue flower, like a small blue star in the green grass.

ABOUT A LITTLE MOUSE NAMED HENRY FRITZELL

Henry Fritzell
That rapscallion mouse
Got out of his cage
And ran out of the house.

He ran down the road
Where the cars never go
And he went to the country,
Singing Hy de O Ho.

He passed a green lake
That was full of fish.
He saw a white horse
And he made a wish,
Singing Hy de O Ho.

But—

When he came
Where the buttercups grow,
He waved all his whiskers
And stood on one toe.

He jumped up and down
And he ran all about.
He peeped and he squeaked
And he squealed in and out.

But after he'd run
Up and down,
All around,
He'd had all his fun
And he longed for the town.

For out in the country
A sleepy young mouse
Who was used to a cage
Could not find a house.

So he ran back the road
Where the cars never go,
And he ran into his house
And his cage
Just so.

And now he's asleep
And the cook doesn't know
He was out of his cage
A short time ago.

THE WONDERFUL DAY

"Whee," said the kittens "what a wonderful day! Whee what a wonderful day!" and they arched their backs and spread their paws and sharpened their claws on the rug.

"Woof," said the big dog "I'm glad I'm awake— Woof what a wonderful day!" And he stretched and yawned and his black eyes were shiny as he woke in the wonderful day.

And all the little birds in the trees whistled and chirped—"The day is young, we are young, the year is young Spring Spring Spring is young. Spring is green. Cheer Cheer Cheer Spring is here!"

But the little boy didn't wake up.

The sun shone in through the window warm and cool. It made the white in the room shiny. A soft breeze blew in the window and ruffled the curls on the little boy's head.

But the little boy didn't wake up.

The birds fluttered their wings outside and the sunlight burned green on the trees.

But the little boy didn't wake up.

The kittens climbed on the little boy's back and blinked their starry eyes.

The old dog sat by the little boy's bed and stared at him right in the face. "I will look him awake," said the old dog, "for he must see this beautiful day."

But the little boy didn't wake up.

Trapper Trapper Trapper chattered the grey squirrel, and his claws went scratching over the roof.

Tack Tack Tack Tack pecked the woodpecker in the old wooden tree.

And a clear note like falling water came from the throat of a bird.

Then the little boy woke up.

THE HEAVENLY DAY

It's a heavenly day
  crowed the rooster
It's a crackerjack day
  cawed the crow

The old sun smiled
  on that heavenly day
A warm smile on the earth below

And the little birds sang
  all over the sky
The winds blew to and fro

It's a heavenly day
  crowed the rooster
It's a crackerjack day
  cawed the crow.